PERSEPHONE

RETOLD AND ILLUSTRATED BY
WARWICK HUTTON

MARGARET K. MCELDERRY BOOKS
New York

MAXWELL MACMILLAN CANADA
Toronto

MAXWELL MACMILLAN INTERNATIONAL
New York · Oxford · Singapore · Sydney

This book is for Joseph

Margaret K. McElderry Books
Macmillan Publishing Company
866 Third Avenue
New York, NY 10022

Maxwell Macmillan Canada, Inc.
1200 Eglinton Avenue East
Suite 200
Don Mills, Ontario M3C 3N1

Macmillan Publishing Company is part of the Maxwell Communication
Group of Companies.
First edition
Printed in Singapore
2 4 6 8 10 9 7 5 3 1
The text of this book is set in Palatino.
The illustrations are rendered in watercolor and pen on paper.

Library of Congress Catalog Card Number: 93-20590
ISBN 0-689-50600-7

The tale of Persephone is also the story of summer and winter, and how they came about. At the beginning of time Zeus, chief of all the gods, ruled over the earth and the heavens. Poseidon was god of the sea and oceans, and Hades was god of the underworld.

It was dark and barren in the underworld. Only a few shafts of light filtered down from the world above. There were no flowers, and no birds sang. Hades could not persuade any nymph or goddess to marry him, for no one wanted to live in the dark and endless winter that was his home. In his loneliness the king of the underworld took to wandering the earth in his black-horsed chariot, looking for a queen to share his kingdom.

One day, when the sky was blue and flowers covered the fields of Sicily, the god of the underworld paused in his search. He got out of his chariot and looked around. Through the trees he saw a wonderful sight. In the middle of a group of nymphs, holding the flowers she had gathered, was the most beautiful woman he had ever seen. It was Persephone, daughter of the goddess Demeter. He would not *ask* her to marry him, Hades thought, for someone who loved flowers so much would not willingly be queen of the underworld.

He walked quickly over to the group of nymphs, and, lifting up Persephone, he carried her back to his chariot. Astonished and frightened, she was too surprised to protest. The nymphs ran off, and Hades drove away at great speed. Persephone's flowers lay scattered on the ground.

Hades knew that the beautiful wife he had found for himself was Demeter's daughter. And he knew Demeter would be furious when she found out what had happened to Persephone, so he drove on as fast as he could back to the underworld.

Soon he reached the river Cyane. The spirits of the river, seeing such a beautiful girl being kidnapped, rose up in anger. A large wave, like a wall of water, threatened the dark chariot. But Hades had the power granted only to gods. With a flourish of his hand he turned and struck open the earth as if it were made of soft cheese. There was a great clap of thunder, and Hades, with his stolen bride, vanished downward to the underworld.

That evening Persephone's mother began to look for her.
All night Demeter called, and all the next day. She was the
goddess of all growing things, and as despair welled up in
her, she forgot her daily duties. No showers of rain came, no
morning dew; the land grew parched, and the corn in the
fields was dry and shriveled.

Meanwhile, below the earth, Persephone pined. In silence she sat at Hades' side. With the world of sun and sky, trees and flowers gone, she felt as if she were dead herself. Hades admired his prize, pleading with her to eat something, but she sat motionless, with tears running down her face, thinking of her lost world above. "Come and see *my* garden," said Hades, trying desperately to please her. He led her to a grove of pomegranate bushes that grew forlornly in the underworld. Absentmindedly Persephone fingered the pomegranates, and as she thought of her mother she wept again.

For nine days Demeter wandered the land above calling for her daughter. Like Persephone she could not eat, and like Persephone she grew thin.

On the tenth day Demeter came to the river Cyane. Here the land was still green, the waters rippled and murmured. And as she walked along its bank, Demeter came to a spring that bubbled out of the rocks into the river.

She sat thoughtfully beside it, and its soft crystal murmurings seemed to talk to her. It was the spirit of the river speaking. Demeter learned how the river had tried to stop Hades with a great wave of water. Then the bubbling spring told of the river's long journey to the sea, and how, when the river ran underground, it had seen Persephone waiting and weeping in the darkness.

At last Demeter knew what had happened. In fury she went to Zeus, chief of all the gods. He had known about Persephone but had done nothing. Then, as he had watched Demeter grieve and neglect all the plants and crops, he had begun to worry. Zeus disliked interfering with the other gods. But he knew that this time he had to do something. He summoned Hermes, messenger of the gods. "I want you to go to the underworld and tell Hades I know he has kidnapped Persephone, and that, if she has eaten nothing while she has been held there, she must be returned to her mother."

The eyes of Hades narrowed thoughtfully when he
heard this message.

For the reunion of mother and daughter Zeus himself appeared, but as Persephone ran into the arms of her mother, Hades looked craftily at her. "Did I not see you eat some seeds from my pomegranates?"

Then Persephone remembered. Without thinking, as she had wandered sadly among the bushes in the underworld garden, she had eaten a few pink seeds from one of the ripe pomegranates. "But I only ate six small seeds!" she cried. Zeus thought long and hard when he heard this. Hades smiled to himself. At last Zeus looked up. "I have decided what to do. Persephone, you can return to your mother now, but because you ate six pomegranate seeds, you must go back to Hades in the underworld for six months of every year."

And that is the way it has been to this day. Spring comes
every year as Persephone rushes back into the arms of her
mother, and all the world grows green again.

As fall approaches and Persephone must return to the underworld, the earth becomes sadder and colder. In winter, nothing grows, for Persephone is then queen of the underworld.

THE END